Happy

HARRY'S

Café

Menu

For Emma, Elsie and Emile, and remembering my father, Harold, who told me a version of this story.
Michael Rosen

First published 2012 by Walker Books Ltd, 87 Vauxhall Walk, London SE11 5HJ

2 4 6 8 10 9 7 5 3 1

Text © 2012 Michael Rosen   Illustrations © 2012 Richard Holland

The right of Michael Rosen and Richard Holland to be identified as author and illustrator respectively of
this work has been asserted by them in accordance with the Copyright, Designs and Patents Act 1988

This book has been typeset in Bodoni poster compressed

Printed in China

British Library Cataloguing in Publication Data:
a catalogue record for this book is available from the British Library

ISBN: 978-1-4063-1446-5

www.walker.co.uk

WALKER BOOKS
AND SUBSIDIARIES
LONDON · BOSTON · SYDNEY · AUCKLAND

For Camilla and Evie   Richard

Michael Rosen

Happy
HARRY'S
Café

illustrated by

Richard Holland

Here's

Harry.

He works at

Happy

HARRY'S

Café.

Harry makes great

soup.

His friends run for Harry's

soup,

before Harry's

soup

runs out.

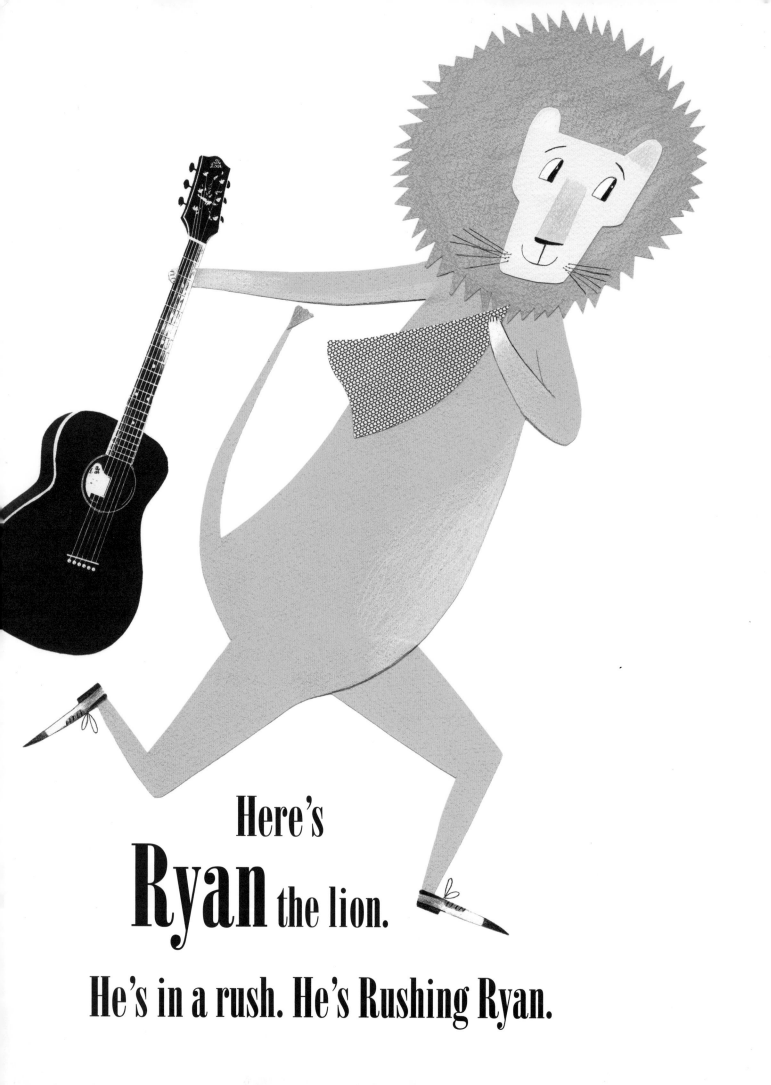

Here's
Ryan the lion.

He's in a rush. He's Rushing Ryan.

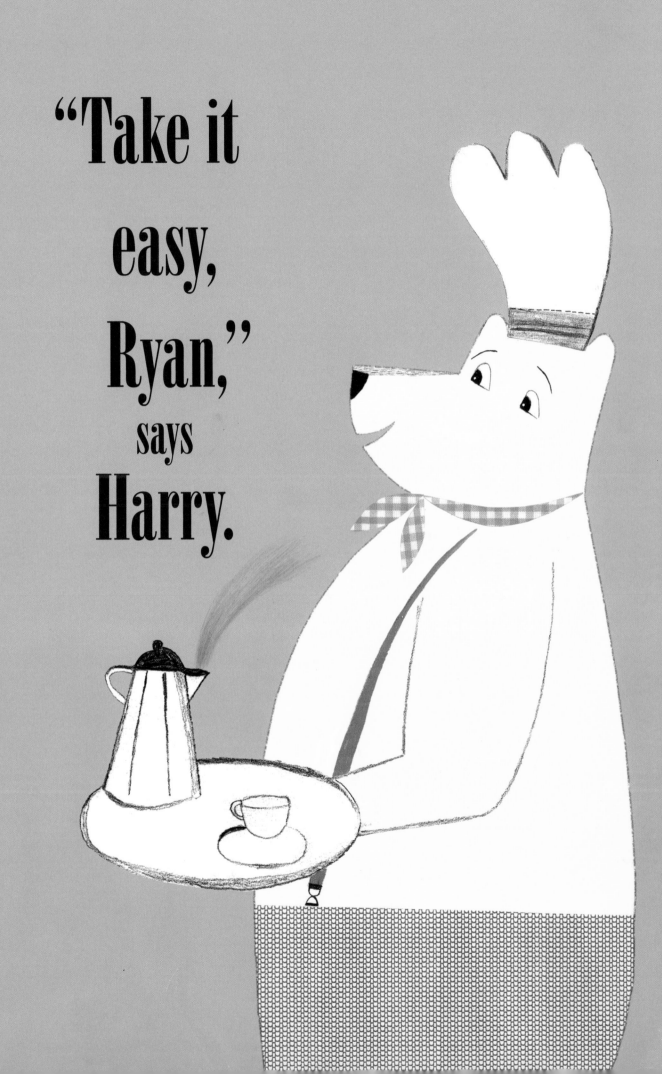

"Take it easy, Ryan," says Harry.

Here's
Jo the crow.

She's riding fast.

Jo's no Slow-Jo, oh no.

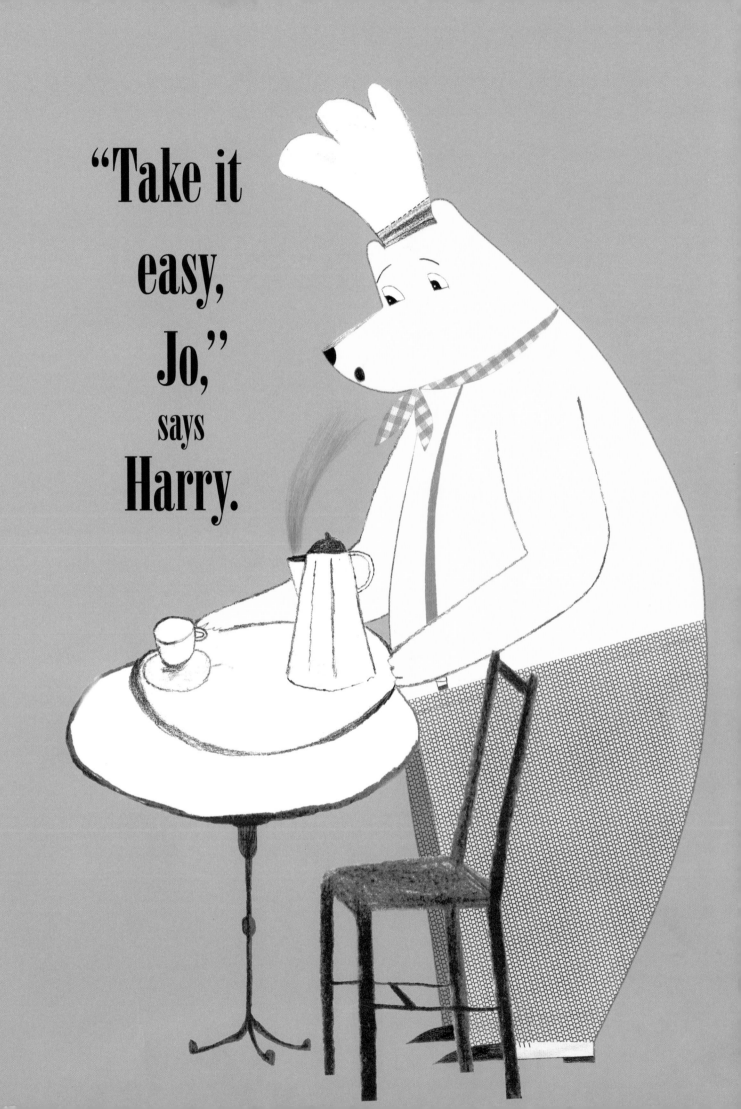

"Take it easy, Jo," says Harry.

Here's
Robin the robin.

Robin is really bobbing along.

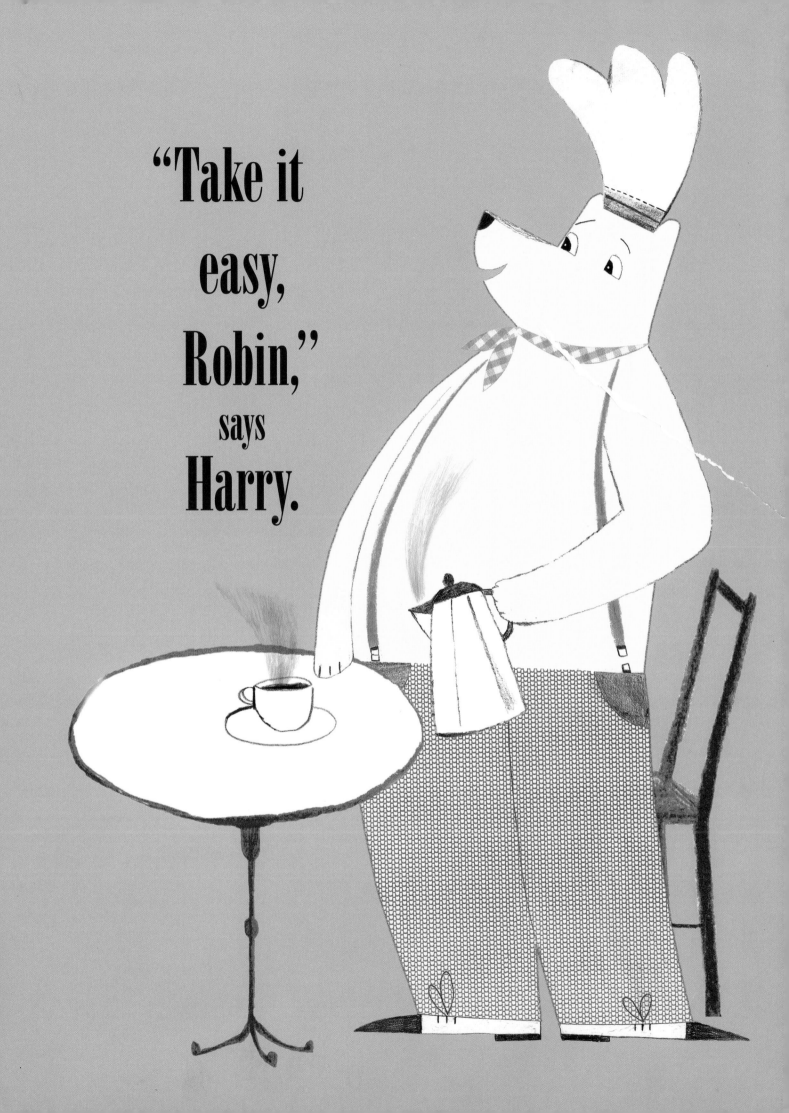

"Take it easy, Robin," says Harry.

Here's
Matt the cat.

As fast as the wind, and faster than that.

"Take it easy, Matt," says Harry.

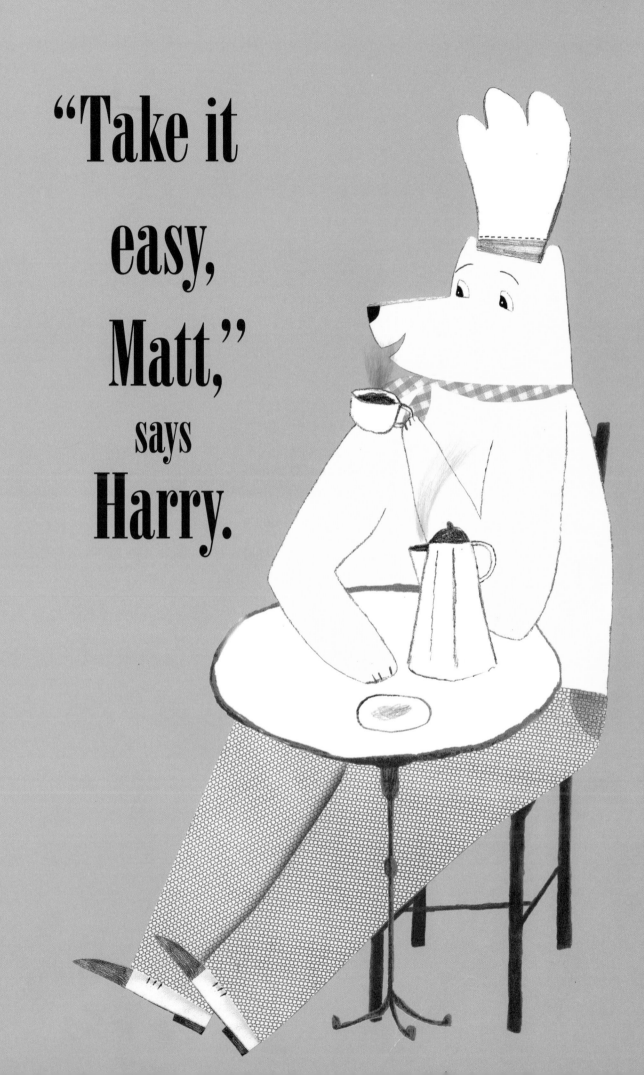

They're all in a hurry to have Harry's **soup.** Everyone **loves** Harry's **soup.**

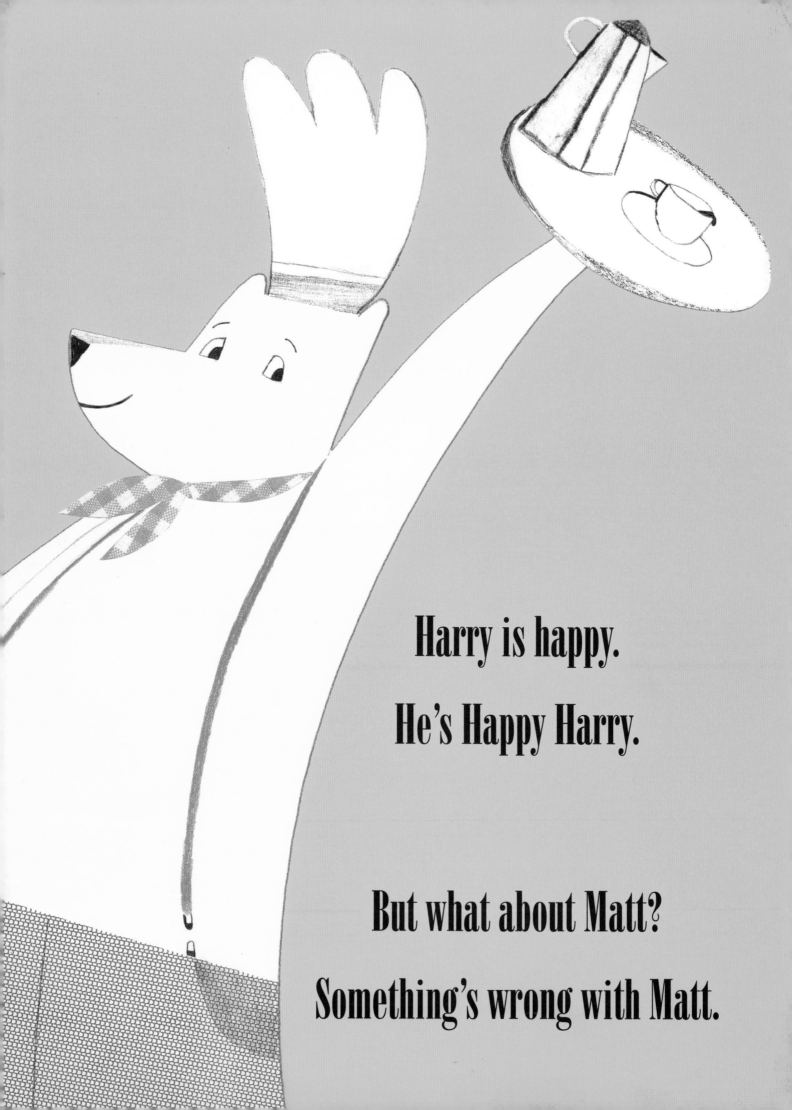

Harry is happy.

He's Happy Harry.

But what about Matt?

Something's wrong with Matt.

"Hey,

Harry,"

says Matt.

"The

soup's

no good."

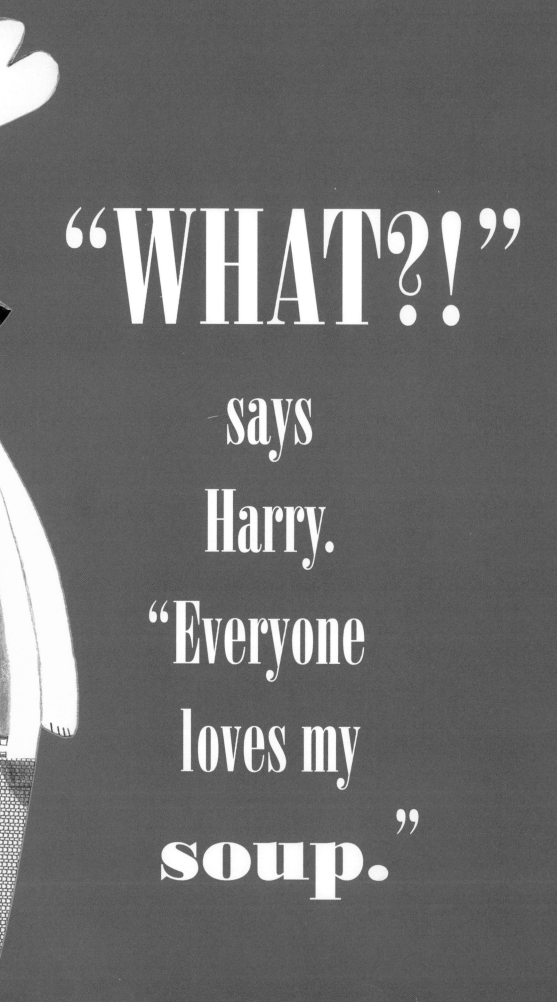

"**WHAT?!**" says Harry. "Everyone loves my **soup.**"

"You come and try it,
Harry,"
says Matt.

"OK, Matt,"

says

Harry.
"I'll try it."

"Hey, Matt," says Harry. "There's no spoon. You haven't got a spoon."

"That's it, Harry!"

says Matt.

"There's no spoon.

I haven't got a spoon.

That's what's wrong with the

soup,

Harry."

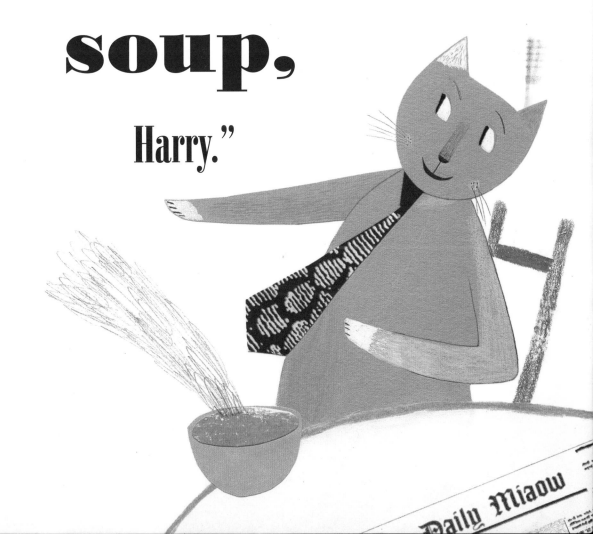

Everyone laughs about the
soup
with no spoon.

Harry gives Matt a spoon.

"You know something?" says Matt.

"What?" says Harry.

"Great

soup,

Harry!"

says Matt.

And...

Harry and **soup**

If you don't have a spoon

If you can't taste the soup

So would I like a spoon?

Do you like the soup?

The soup is good.

The soup is good.

The soup is good.

Matt sing a
song:

you can't taste the soup.

the soup's no good.

Oh yes I would.

Oh the soup is good.

The soup is good.

The soup is good.

The soup is good.

Everyone joined in
and everyone was happy at

Happy

HARRY'S

Café.